In darkness there is death.

-Eric Van Lustbader

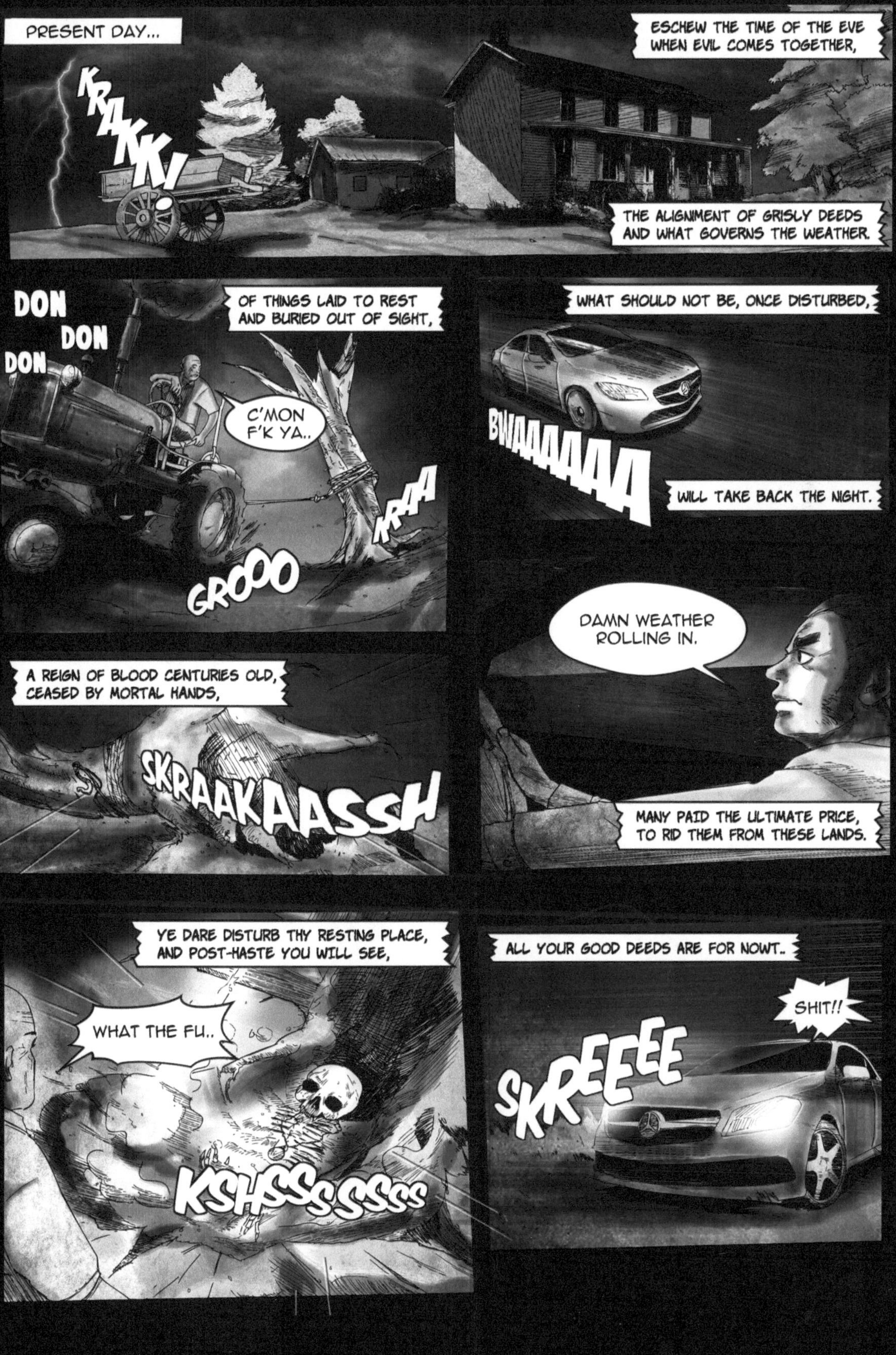

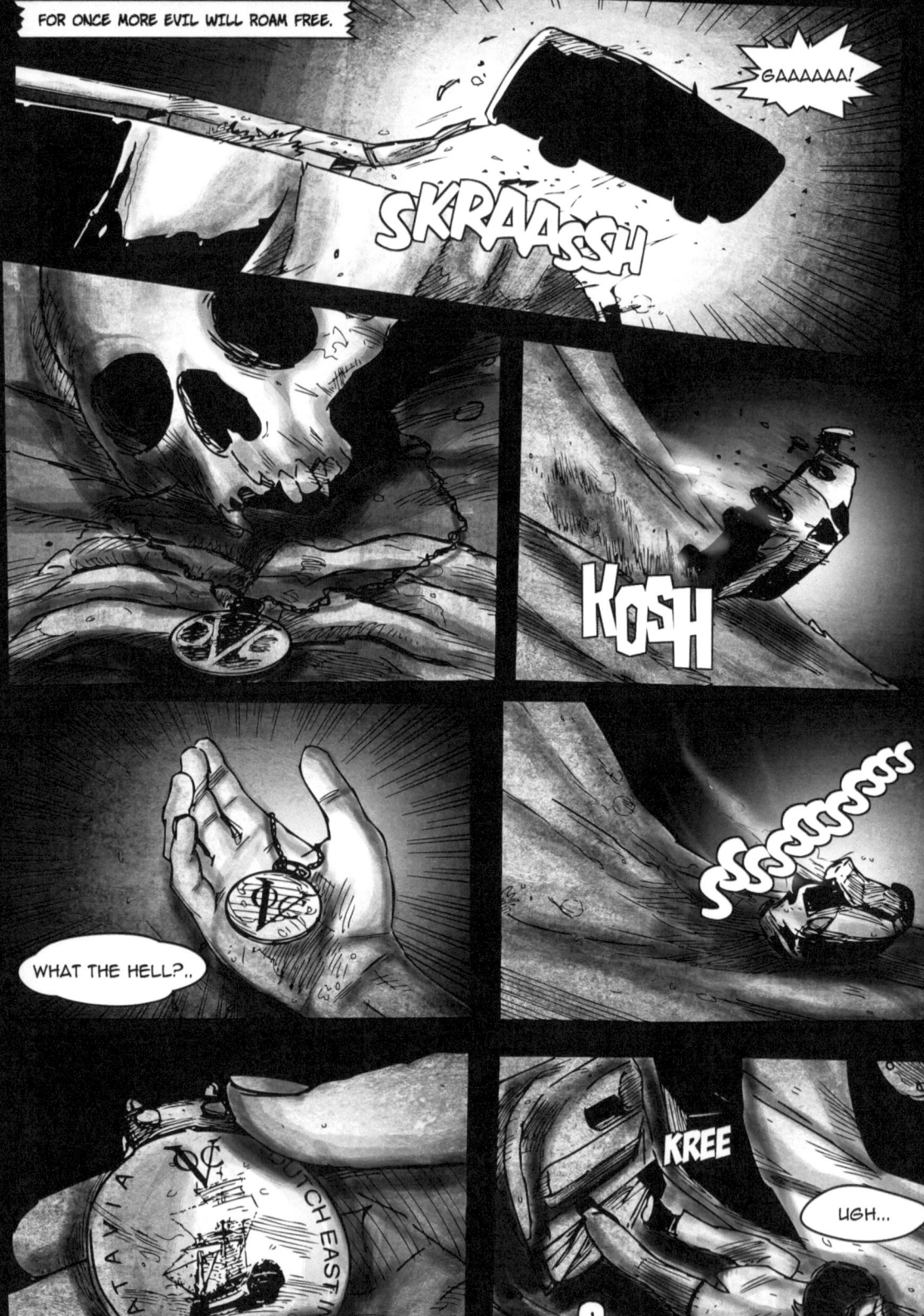

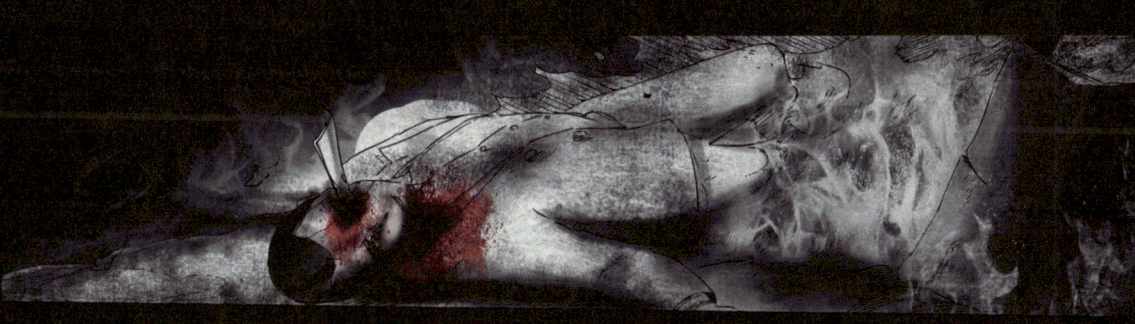

WESTERN AUSTRALIAN MARITIME MUSEUM, LATER THAT DAY..

LOOK, IF YOUR SHIT ISN'T OUT OF MY PLACE BY FRIDAY, I'M THROWING IT INTO THE STREET! DON'T YOU DARE TRY CALLING ME AGAIN! WE ARE DONE YOU USELESS FUCK!

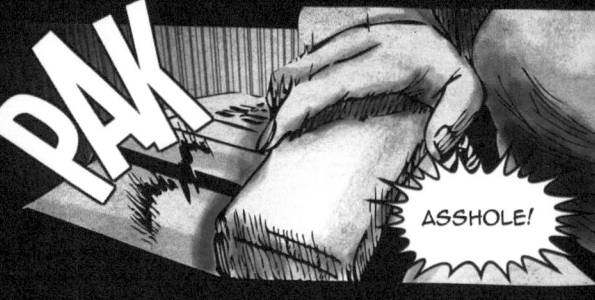

ASSHOLE!

YOU ALRIGHT KATE?

YEAH, FANTASTIC. THE BASTARD HAD BEEN STEALING FROM ME FOR MONTHS SO HE COULD GET HIGH WITH HIS SLUT ON THE SIDE.

CAN'T BELIEVE I THOUGHT I COULD MAKE IT WORK. I'M SO STUPID.

NO.. HE'S JUST..

BIP BIP BIP

JESUS CHRIST.. SERIOUSLY!?

LISTEN HERE YOU MOTHERFUCKER.. ENOUGH WITH THE HARASSMENT!

I'M CALLING THE POLICE!!

ERM.. I CAN POSSIBLY SAVE YOU SOME TIME MISS.

THIS IS SARGEANT RICHARDSON OF THE W.A. POLICE..

AM I SPEAKING TO KATE LEE?

OH! I'M SO SORRY.. I JUST..

..YES.. THIS IS KATE.

OK, LOOK KATE.. I'M GETTING IN TOUCH WITH YOU BECAUSE YOU'RE A CURATOR FOR MARITIME ARCHAEOLOGY.

A SKELETON WAS UNEARTHED THE OTHER DAY, AND ALONG WITH IT, A MEDALLION THAT MAY BE OF SOME INTEREST TO YOU...

GOOD, SEE YOU TOMORROW.

OH.. OKAY.. TELL ME MORE. RIGHT.. WHAT?

YES.. OKAY. THAT'S FINE.

???

I CAN'T GO ALONE..

JENNY

DIT DIT DOO DOO

DOO DIT DIT DIT DOO

DOO DIT DIT DOO DIT DIT DOO DIT DIT

STEVE, MY PHONE..

LEAVE IT.

DIT DIT DIT DOO DIT DOO

IT'S KATE.

DOO DIT DIT

WELL DON'T FUCKIN' ANSWER IT!

DOO DIT DIT DIT DIT DOO DIT DOO DOO DIT

LOOK, SHE'S BEEN GOING THROUGH SOME SHIT LATELY.. AND SHE NEEDS MY SUPPORT!

BLIP

HI KATE. HOW ARE THINGS?

BETTER. IT'S DONE. WE'RE FINISHED. HE LOST HIS SHIT, AND SO DID I, BUT IT'S DONE.

THAT'S GREAT. HOW ARE YOU FEELING?

LIKE SHIT. LOOK, I'M GOING TO GET AWAY FOR A FEW DAYS, HEAD OUT TO THE COUNTRYSIDE. THERE'S BEEN A FIND I WANT TO LOOK AT.

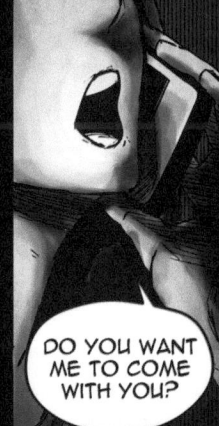

DO YOU WANT ME TO COME WITH YOU?

COULD YOU? I COULD USE THE COMPANY. I DON'T REALLY FEEL LIKE BEING ALONE.

TELL THAT BITCH YOU'RE NOT GOING ANYWHERE WITHOUT ME! I KNOW WHAT SHE'S LIKE AND I DON'T TRUST THE TWO OF YOU ALONE TOGETHER!

WHAT?!

LIKE HE CAN FUCKING TALK!

ALRIGHT. BUT HE'D BETTER NOT PISS ME OFF. I'M IN THE MOOD FOR MURDER AND THERE'S A LOT OF PLACES TO HIDE A BODY WHERE WE'RE GOING.

LOOK, IT'S BETTER NOW.

KATE, HE WON'T LET ME GO UNLESS HE COMES ALONG. IT'LL BE FINE.

PICK YOU UP AT 7AM.

OK. BYE.

BYE.

EAST COAST. HEAD OFFICE OF TETSUCHEM LTD.

..AND HERE'S THE REPORT FROM THE WEST, BOSS.

..IT OCCURED ON ONE OF THE STATE'S MOST NOTORIOUS STRETCHES OF ROAD.

JODY FEWSTER JOINS US NOW, LIVE FROM THE SCENE.

..HOW ABOUT SHARING WITH US EXACTLY WHERE WE'RE GOING, AND WHY?

SURE.

WELL, YOU BOTH KNOW THE STORY OF THE BATAVIA, RIGHT?

OF COURSE!

NO. TELL ME.

OK. WE'VE GOT TIME.

HOPE YOU'RE READY FOR THIS..

..IT'S ONE HELL OF A STORY.

IN 1628, A DUTCH SHIP, THE BATAVIA, LEFT THE NETHERLANDS BOUND FOR THE DUTCH EAST INDIES. ON BOARD WERE OVER 300 MEN, WOMEN AND CHILDREN, AND A HUGE AMOUNT OF GOLD AND SILVER FOR TRADE.

THOUSANDS GATHERED AT THE PORT IN TEXEL TO BID THEM A SAFE JOURNEY.

NO ONE COULD HAVE POSSIBLY IMAGINED THE HORRORS THAT LAY AHEAD.

SEVERAL MONTHS INTO THE JOURNEY, AFTER STOPPING AT CAPE TOWN FOR SUPPLIES, THE SKIPPER DELIBERATELY STEERED THE SHIP OFF COURSE.

KSHHH

THIS WAS ALL PART OF A PLOT HE HAD CONTRIVED WITH A PSYCHOPATHIC GENIUS NAMED JERONIMUS CORNELISZ.

THEY, ALONG WITH SEVERAL OTHERS ON BOARD HAD PLANNED A MUTINY WHICH WOULD SEE THEM TAKE THE SHIP ALONG WITH ALL ITS GOLD AND SILVER.

IN 1629 ON JUNE THE 4TH THE SHIP STRUCK A REEF ON A GROUP OF ISLANDS OFF THE WEST COAST OF AUSTRALIA.

ABSOLUTE CHAOS ENSUED AND A MAD SCRAMBLE WAS MADE FOR THE SHIP'S LONGBOAT AND YAWL.

OF THE 322 ABOARD, 40 DROWNED.

THE REMAINING SURVIVORS MANAGED TO DRAG THEMSELVES ASHORE.

A VERY BASIC CAMP WAS SET UP ON THE ISLAND WITH WHATEVER THEY COULD SALVAGE FROM THE WRECKAGE.

THE HOT DAYS WERE UNFORGIVING.

THERE WAS NO FRESH WATER ON ANY OF THE ISLANDS.

AFTER UNSUCCESSFULLY SCOURING THE MAINLAND FOR WATER, COMMANDER PAELSART AND SOME SELECT CREW MEMBERS TOOK THEIR 30 FOOT LONGBOAT ON A 33 DAY JOURNEY TO INDONESIA TO SEEK HELP. INCREDIBLY, EVERYONE ABOARD SURVIVED.

WHILE THE COMMANDER WAS AWAY, CORNELISZ AND HIS BAND OF FOLLOWERS SEIZED THEIR CHANCE TO TAKE OVER.

WHAT ENSUED NEXT WAS THE STUFF OF NIGHTMARES AS THE BLOODTHIRSTY ENCLAVE TOOK OVER AND BEGAN THEIR REIGN OF TERROR.

THOSE WHO PROTESTED WERE SLAUGHTERED.

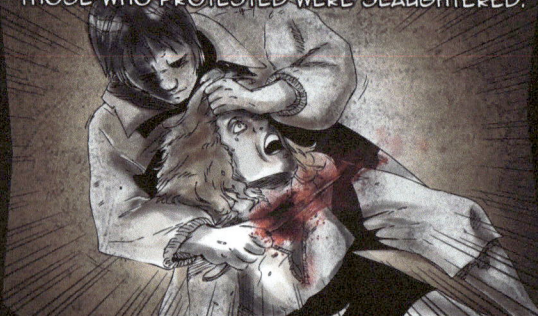

OTHERS WHO REFUSED TO FOLLOW CORNELISZ HAD THEIR SKULLS SMASHED IN OR WERE DROWNED IN THE COLD SEA.

THERE WERE ALSO TALES OF CANNIBALISIM AND VIOLENT ACTS OF DEPRAVITY.

THE RAPES WERE HORRIFIC AND CONSTANT WITH FEMALES KEPT ALIVE FOR THE SOLE PURPOSE OF BECOMING SEX SLAVES.

FIGHTING BACK COULD ONLY DO SO MUCH.

AS THE NUMBERS OF SADISTIC FOLLOWERS INCREASED, THE OTHERS HAD NO CHOICE BUT TO FALL INTO SUBMISSION.

CORNELISZ OWNED THEM ALL.

UNFORTUNATELY FOR HIM, PELSAERT RETURNED.

UPON LEARNING OF THE MASSACRE, PELSAERT ORDERED HIS TROOPS TO CAPTURE CORNELISZ AND HIS MEN.

A BLOODY BATTLE ENSUED.

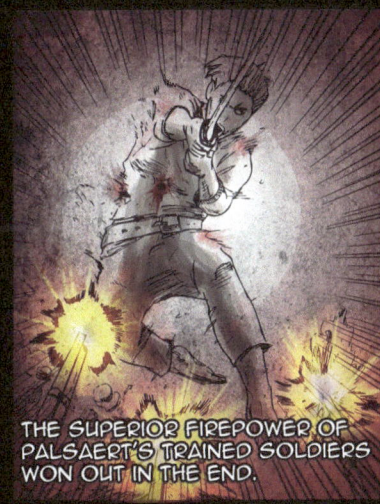

THE SUPERIOR FIREPOWER OF PALSAERT'S TRAINED SOLDIERS WON OUT IN THE END.

THOSE WHO SURVIVED WERE CAPTURED.

A DECISION WAS MADE TO HOLD A TRIAL ON THE ISLAND AS TRANSPORTING AND SECURING THE ACCUSED WOULD HAVE BEEN IMPOSSIBLE DUE TO THE LIMITED ROOM ON THE RESCUE VESSELS.

THE WORST OF THE OFFENDERS WERE STRAPPED TO A LARGE WAGON WHEEL..

..AND THEN BRUTALLY BEATEN UNTIL ALL OF THEIR BONES WERE SMASHED AND SHATTERED.

THIS FORM OF PUNISHMENT WAS KNOWN AS,

IT WAS THE MOST SEVERE FORM OF PUNISHMENT TO BE SUBJECTED TO AT THE TIME. HOWEVER..

'BEING BROKEN ON THE WHEEL'

..EVEN AFTER A HORRIFIC BEATING, SOME REFUSED TO DIE. IT WAS ONLY ONCE A STAKE WAS DRIVEN THROUGH THEIR HEART THAT THEY WOULD FINALLY SUCCOMBE TO DEATH.

OTHERS HAD THEIR HANDS CHOPPED OFF..

..AND WERE THEN HUNG AND LEFT FOR THE BIRDS.

EVEN WITH A BROKEN NECK, SOME CONTINUED TO SCREAM FOR HOURS.

ONLY TWO WERE SPARED.

CONSIDERED MINOR OFFENDERS, THEY WERE GIVEN A MEAGER AMOUNT OF FOOD AND WATER, AND WERE TOLD TO MAKE THEIR WAY TO THE DESOLATE MAINLAND.

WHAT BECAME OF THEM IS UNKNOWN.

THEY WERE NEVER HEARD FROM AGAIN.

WHAT A LOAD OF SHIT.

I THOUGHT YOU LIKED STORIES WITH RAPE AND MURDER.

THE MURDER I CAN DO WITHOUT..

SQUEEZE

THE RAPE HOWEVER HAS TURNED ME ON!

GET YOUR FUCKING HANDS OFF ME YOU ASSHOLE!

AFTERNOON.

RRRRRRRRRRMMM

SKRUNCH

AFTERNOON.

RICHARDSON TOLD ME YOU WERE ON YOUR WAY OVER.

WE SAW WHAT YOU FOUND. VERY INTERESTING INDEED. WOULD YOU MIND SHOWING US WHERE YOU FOUND IT?

NOT AT ALL.

THE POLICE AND THEIR FORENSICS CAME. TOOK ALL THE BONES AND SPENT AGES EXCAVATING FURTHER.

DID THEY FIND MUCH ELSE?

NOPE.

THEY SAID IT WAS THE STRANGEST SKELETON THEY HAD EVER SEEN.

WHY'S THAT?

TEETH LIKE A DOG THEY RECKON.

AND THE BONES.

VERY WELL PRESERVED AFTER BEING BURIED FOR SO LONG.

LIKE A DOG?

YEP.

BULLSHIT.

LOOK, I THINK THERE'S MORE TO THIS THAN YOU KNOW.

ME NAN USED TO TALK ABOUT CREATURES LIKE THIS.. I FIGURED SHE WAS JUST GOING SENILE.

ACCORDING TO HER THEY HAVE A HISTORY AROUND THESE PARTS.

COME INSIDE AND MEET HER. SHE'D LOVE THE COMPANY. WE DON'T OFTEN GET VISITORS.

UP ON THE HILL.. NOT FAR AWAY.
VVVRRRRRRMMMSSHH
CAREFUL.
I KNOW.
KSSH
HMM.. THERE'S SOMETHING GOING ON OVER THERE.
DO YOU THINK IT'S THE GIRL?
I THINK THE ONLY WAY TO KNOW IS TO HEAD OVER THERE AND FIND OUT.
SOON..
WELL LOOK AT THIS.
LOOKS LIKE A STORM IS ROLLING IN.
FAMOUS LAST WORDS.
WE'LL BE ALRIGHT.
PULL YOUR FUCKIN' HEAD IN.

INSIDE..

TAKE A SEAT. SHE'LL BE OUT IN A MINUTE

CAN I USE YOUR TOILET? PLEASE?

SURE. JUST DOWN THE HALL. TAKE CARE.

TAKE CARE? WEIRD. HOLY CRAP.

SPOOKY LOOKING FAMILY. THAT WOMAN LOOKS LIKE SHE COULD HAVE BEEN KATE'S GRANDMOTHER.

I WONDER IF..

SSSSH

HELLO DEAR.

SHIT!

OH! HI.. I'M JEN.

LOVELY TO MEET YOU DEAR. PLEASE EXCUSE THE STATE OF THE PLACE. IT'S NOT OFTEN WE GET VISITORS UP HERE.

YOU HAVE A LOVELY HOME. THANK YOU FOR LETTING US VISIT.

PRRRRL

SO, WHAT BRINGS YOU ALL THE WAY OUT HERE?

WHAT CAN YOU TELL US ABOUT THE HISTORY OF THIS AREA?

I'LL TELL YOU WHAT I THINK YOU WANT TO HEAR ABOUT.

WHEN I WAS A LITTLE GIRL THERE WAS A SMALL, YET TIGHT COMMUNITY THRIVING IN THESE HILLS.

EVERYONE KNEW EVERYONE.

SADLY, ONE SUMMER PEOPLE STARTED TO GO MISSING AND THE SAFE LITTLE HAVEN WE HAD ALL ENJOYED WAS FOREVER SHATTERED.

THE SCENES OF THE DISAPPEARANCES WERE EXTREMELY GRUESOME. IT WAS AS IF A WILD BEAST WAS ON THE LOOSE.

NO ONE KNEW WHAT TO DO, OR WHO WOULD BE NEXT.

THEN, LATE ONE NIGHT, MY SISTER WAS TAKEN.

IMMEDIATELY, A SEARCH PARTY WAS FORMED AND SET OFF INTO THE FOREST.

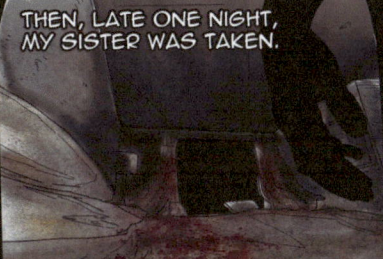

THEY SOON CAME ACROSS THE BEAST,

KLAAAM

AND MY FATHER BLEW ITS FACE OFF.

THEY BROUGHT MY SISTER'S TORN UP BODY HOME.

SHE WASN'T EXPECTED TO SURVIVE THE NIGHT.

HOWEVER..

..SHE DID.

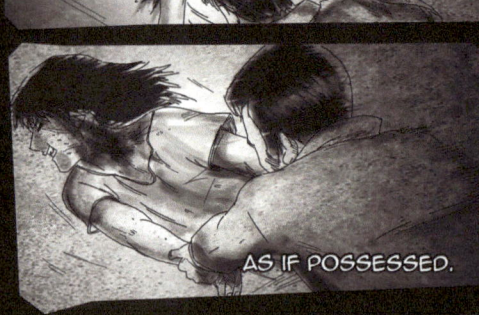

SHE BECAME HORRIBLY VIOLENT.

AS IF POSSESSED.

THEY CHAINED HER UP,

SHE WAS FAR TOO DANGEROUS.

SHE HAD BECOME ONE OF, THEM.

BUT IT WASN'T ENOUGH.

TO APPEASE THE REST OF THE VILLAGE, WE TOLD THEM SHE HAD DIED,

AND THEN HAD A FUNERAL IN THE YARD.

SO, THAT'S THE SKELETON THAT WAS FOUND OUTSIDE?
OH GOODNESS NO!
HUH? SO, WHO IS IT?
NO IDEA. AN EMPTY COFFIN WAS BURIED OUT THERE.
MY SISTER WAS BURIED UNDER THE FLOORBOARDS. RIGHT WHERE WE'RE SITTING.
WHAT?!
MEANWHILE..
SNAP!
DID YOU HEAR..
WHAT THE FUCK?!!
TH..TH..THEY'RE ALL AROUND US!
LOOK OUT!!
GNNNNNN!!

STOP!

KSSSSSH

WHO GOES THERE?!

DON'T SHOOT!

PLEASE.

HENRY! PUT THE GUN DOWN! THEY'RE UNARMED!

WHAT ARE YOU DOING ON MY LAND!?

WHO ARE YOU?

LOOK, YOU'RE WASTING YOUR TIME IF YOU THINK WE'RE THE THREAT HERE. THERE ARE SOME CREATURES OUT THERE THAT COULD BE COMING THIS WAY.

IF YOU'VE GOT ANY SENSE YOU'LL HELP US ALL GET OUT OF HERE!

WHAT CREATURES!? BULLSHIT!

BLOODTHIRSTY UNDEAD, THEY'LL KILL YOU ALL.

OUT OF MY WAY!

NO! YOU MUSTN'T DISTURB THEM!

SEEMS LIKE THEY'VE ALREADY BEEN DISTURBED.

TIME TO FIND OUT IF THERE'S ANY TRUTH TO YOUR TALE.

KSSHAAAA

AND GET A BIT OF PAYBACK AT THE SAME TIME.

HENRY! NO! PLEASE DON'T DO IT!

THIS IS ABSOLUTE BULLSHIT. THERE'S NOTHING OUT THERE.

AM I THE ONLY SANE ONE HERE?

YOU THINK WE'RE FULL OF SHIT DO YOU?

THEN WHY NOT HEAD OUT THERE AND SEE FOR YOURSELF TOUGH GUY?

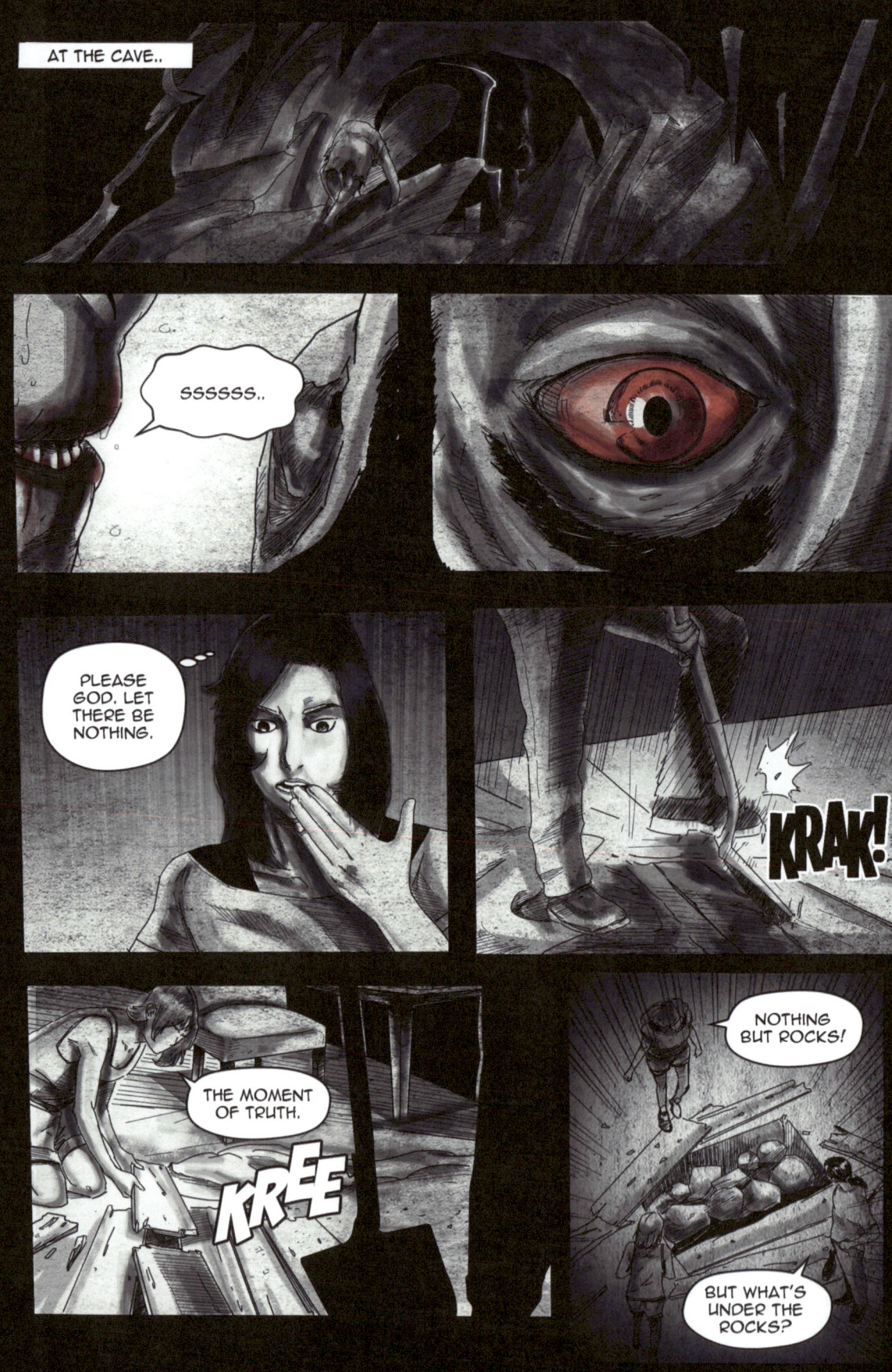

KSSSSSH

OH DEAR.

UUNGH!

LOOKS LIKE IT IS JUST ROCKS!

NO..

DEARS..

KREEE

DON

KRASH

THERE'S SOMETHING HERE!

STOP IT!

YOU DON'T KNOW WHAT YOU'RE MESSING WITH!

SHUT UP YOU OLD BAT!

IT'S NOTHING BUT OLD PLANKS AND OTHER SHIT.

YOU REALLY DONT REMEMBER DO YOU?

REMEMBER WHAT?

YOUR FAMILY.

NO.. I DON'T.

TEN YEARS AGO I WAS FOUND NAKED IN THE FOREST BY A GROUP OF HIKERS.

I DON'T REMEMBER ANYTHING AT ALL BEFORE THAT.

MY FATHER TOLD ME.

TOLD YOU WHAT?

AFTER STEPHANIE WAS TAKEN, YOU WENT TO THE LAIR FOR REVENGE..

YOU NEVER CAME BACK.

GOOD LORD. I REMEMBER NOW.

THEY RAPED ME AND FED OFF ME.

THEIR LEADER SAVED ME.

HE TOOK CARE OF ME.

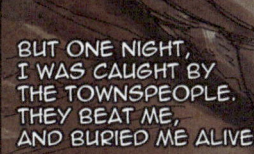

BUT ONE NIGHT, I WAS CAUGHT BY THE TOWNSPEOPLE. THEY BEAT ME, AND BURIED ME ALIVE.

BUT NOW I'M BACK. BACK WITH MY FAMILY.

SOUNDS LIKE THE OLD MAN HAS FOUND OUR FRIENDS.

HURRY UP! THEY'LL BE COMING!

WHAT A SHIT-SHOW. I SHOULD NEVER HAVE AGREED TO COME AND FIND YOU.

COME AND FIND ME?

WHO ARE YOU?

IT DOESN'T MATTER. MY BOSS TOLD ME TO COME AND GET YOU, SO THAT'S WHAT I'M DOING.

YOU'RE FROM THE LAB!

I'M NOT GOING BACK THERE!

LOOK, I DON'T KNOW ANYTHING ABOUT NO LAB. I'M JUST DOING A JOB. NOW, YOU CAN EITHER STICK WITH ME, OR TAKE YOUR CHANCES WITH THE THINGS OUT THERE.. YOUR CHOICE!

÷SOB÷

PLEASE DON'T TAKE ME BACK THERE.

YOU HAVE NO IDEA WHAT HORRIBLE THINGS THEY DO.

LOOK, IF I CAN'T GET THIS THING STARTED, WE'RE NOT GOING ANYWHERE.

IN THE HOUSE..

KATE, YOU'RE SCARING THE SHIT OUT OF ME. WHAT THE FUCK IS GOING ON?

I'M SO SORRY JENNY.

MY GIRL IS STILL HUNGRY.

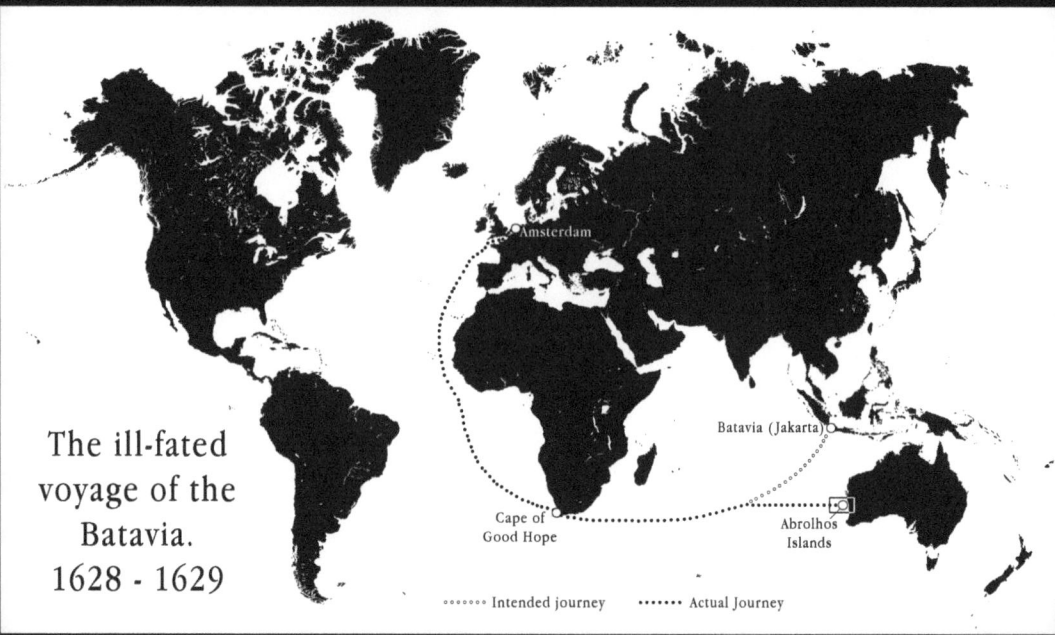

The ill-fated
voyage of the
Batavia.
1628 - 1629

Amsterdam

Batavia (Jakarta)

Cape of
Good Hope

Abrolhos
Islands

⊙⊙⊙⊙⊙ Intended journey ⋯⋯ Actual Journey

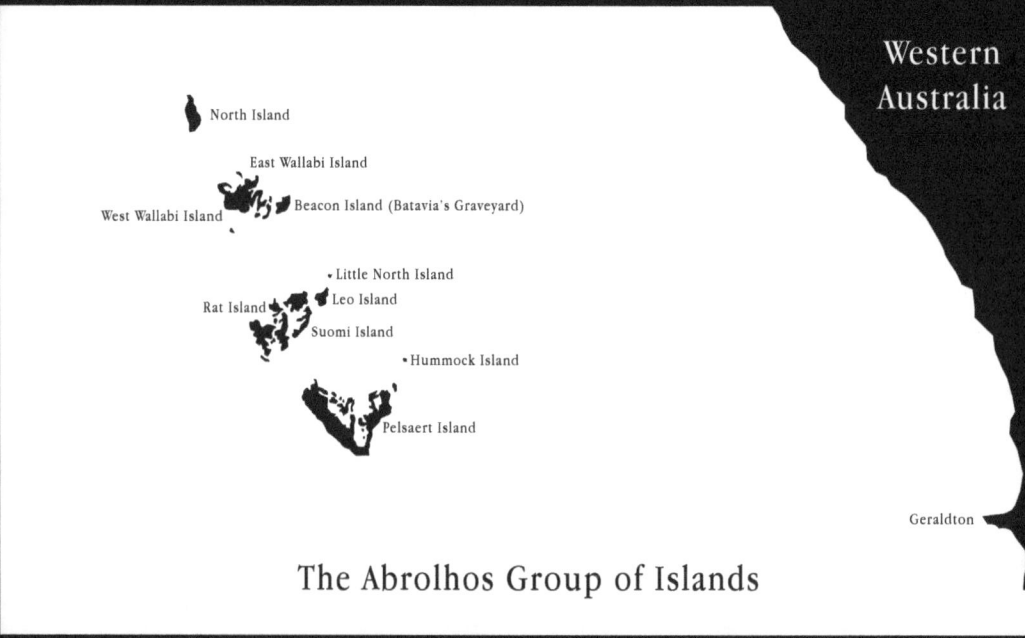

Western
Australia

North Island

East Wallabi Island

West Wallabi Island Beacon Island (Batavia's Graveyard)

• Little North Island
Leo Island

Rat Island

Suomi Island

• Hummock Island

Pelsaert Island

Geraldton

The Abrolhos Group of Islands

For further reading on the Batavia head to: museum.wa.gov.au

www.ingramcontent.com/pod-product-compliance
Lightning Source LLC
Chambersburg PA
CBHW041000170626
46815CB00002B/88